DISNEY·PIXAR
RATATOUILLE
(rat·a·too·ee)

A READ-ALOUD STORYBOOK

Adapted by
Katherine Emmons and Mary Olin

Illustrated by
Ron Cohee, Mara Damiani, Caroline Egan, Mike Inman, Seung Kim,
Maria Elena Naggi, Scott Tilley, and Valeria Turati

Designed by
Tony Fejeran and Stuart Smith of Disney Publishing's Global Design Group

Inspired by the art and character designs created by Pixar

Random House 🏠 New York

Copyright © 2007 Disney Enterprises, Inc./Pixar. All rights reserved. Published in the United States by Random House Children's Books,
a division of Random House, Inc., New York, and in Canada by Random House of Canada Limited, Toronto, in conjunction
with Disney Enterprises, Inc. RANDOM HOUSE and colophon are registered trademarks of Random House, Inc.
Library of Congress Control Number: 2006940314   ISBN: 978-0-7364-2440-0

www.randomhouse.com/kids/disney

Printed in the United States of America

10 9 8 7 6 5 4 3 2 1

In a little cottage in the French countryside, a colony of rats lived in the cozy attic of an old woman named Mabel. Mabel's compost heap was important to the rats, for that was where they chose their evening meal each and every day.

One of those rats had an amazing sense of smell. His name was Remy. Because of his talent, Remy was given an important job: to smell the food and make sure it was safe to eat.

But Remy had a much bigger dream than to sniff garbage. He really wanted to be a chef— the best **gourmet chef** in all of France!

Django, Remy's dad, was proud of his son just the way he was. "You've helped a noble cause," he said one night at dinner in the attic of the cottage.

"Noble? We're stealing garbage," said Remy.

"It isn't stealing if no one wants it," Django argued.

Remy knew that his dad would never understand his dream of working with fine food. Remy also knew that Django wouldn't approve of his sneaking into Mabel's kitchen. Humans were **dangerous**!

So Remy kept his kitchen explorations a secret.

One day, Remy found a beautiful, tasty-looking mushroom. He wanted to hide it until he had time to make it into a **great meal**.

As usual, Emile helped his older brother—though he didn't understand Remy's habits, like walking on two legs instead of four. It had something to do with keeping his front paws **clean** for cooking and eating.

Suddenly, Remy sniffed out
something delicious in Emile's bag.
"Cheese? You found *cheese*?" It
would be a perfect addition to the
mushroom. It just needed to be
cooked. But where? How?

The chimney! "Yeah. Come on!"
Remy yelled to Emile as they
scrambled to the rooftop. But as
Remy happily heated the mushroom
and cheese over the chimney,
Emile spotted a storm coming.
Zap!
Lightning struck the antenna
next to the brothers.

"I know what
this needs!" said
Remy after he tasted
his mushroom creation.
He dragged Emile
straight to Mabel's kitchen!
"Don't like it," Emile said
nervously as Remy showed him
Anyone Can Cook!, the cookbook
written by his hero, Auguste Gusteau.
"Wait a minute. You **read**?"
Emile asked.
If their father only knew! Rats weren't
supposed to read . . . or cook!

"Saffron, saffron," hummed Remy, looking for the spice to make his mushroom perfect. "Gusteau swears by it."

Then Remy heard Gusteau's cooking show on the TV, so he went into the living room to watch. To Remy's dismay, he learned that Gusteau had died from a broken heart. Some said it was because his restaurant had slipped from its five-star status.

Remy felt so sad that he didn't notice Mabel **waking up**. . . .

"Ahhhhh!" Mabel screamed.

The brother rats had to escape the angry, frightened old woman—and fast! After a chaotic chase, the ceiling cracked and began to fall apart.

Django took charge as all the rats plunged from the attic. "Sound the alarm! Evacuate!"

Taking a risk, Remy went back for the cookbook.

The rest of the rats
made it to the creek and
launched their evacuation boats.
"Is everybody here?" shouted
Django. "Do we have everybody?
Where's Remy?"

"I'm coming!" called Remy as he
threw the book into the water and
hopped onto it.

"Give him something to grab on to," ordered Django as the rats floated into the sewer. But Remy didn't make it. He got **separated** from his family and ended up on a wild ride down the sewer rapids.

Alone, exhausted, and soaked, Remy finally found a place to sit down. Where was his family? What would he do? All he had was Auguste Gusteau's cookbook.

Suddenly, a sprightly Gusteau seemed to come to life on a page in the book. Remy couldn't tell if he was crazy or **imagining** Gusteau. But he was glad to have someone to talk to!

"I've just lost my family. All my friends. Probably forever," Remy told Gusteau.

"If you focus on what you've left behind, you will never be able to see what lies ahead." Gusteau smiled encouragingly. "Now, go up and look around."

So Remy climbed up and up until he reached a rooftop and **saw** . . .

"Paris? All this time I've been underneath Paris? Wow!" cried Remy, his breath taken away. "It's beautiful!"

"The *most* beautiful." Gusteau sighed.

Remy looked to his left. His jaw dropped. Gusteau was right next to him . . . on a sign . . . for Gusteau's restaurant!

"Your restaurant?" Remy said to Gusteau. "You've led me to your restaurant!"

For Remy, it was a **dream** come true!

At that moment, a young
man named Linguini arrived at
the restaurant, asking for a job.
He held out a letter from his mother,
who had been an old friend of Gusteau's.
Skinner, the nasty little chef in
charge, was **furious**!
Now he had to let the clumsy young
man work as a garbage boy
in his kitchen.

Meanwhile, Remy had made his way to a skylight in the roof of the restaurant.

Gusteau appeared again. "Let us see how much you know, eh? Which one is the chef?" he quizzed. Remy quickly pointed out Skinner.

"Now, who's that?" Gusteau pointed to Linguini.

"He's nobody," replied Remy. "He doesn't cook."

"What do I always say?" asked Gusteau.

"Anyone can cook!"

The two watched in horror as Linguini accidentally spilled some soup and secretly began concocting an awful replacement. Remy wanted Gusteau to stop the disaster, but Gusteau shrugged. "What can I do? I'm a figment of your imagination."

"But he's ruining the soup! We've got to tell someone that he's—" Suddenly, the skylight opened, and Remy fell right into the kitchen, landing in a sink of dishwater.

The little rat climbed out and ran, but he found no safe hiding place. He had to escape!

Human chefs would never allow a rat in a restaurant kitchen!

But as Remy made a dash for the window, he smelled Linguini's **horrible** soup.

"You know how to fix it," Gusteau said, encouraging him.

Remy jumped to the stove top and adjusted the flame. He added more water and grabbed some spices. *Quickly, now!* He tossed in some more ingredients. It was starting to smell **good**!

Suddenly, a huge face was staring at him. It was Linguini!

When Skinner approached—**slam!**—Linguini trapped Remy under a colander. "How dare you cook in my kitchen?" Skinner yelled at Linguini, and fired him!

But Linguini was more concerned about the soup. He tried to stop the waiter, but he was too late. The soup was whisked off to the dining room, where an important restaurant critic sat waiting. She tasted a spoonful . . . and loved it!

Skinner couldn't believe it, so he tasted the soup himself. **Delicious**.

Reluctantly, Skinner decided to give Linguini another chance. "You will make the soup again, and this time, I'll be paying attention."

In the commotion, Remy popped out from under the colander and made a move for the window. But Skinner spotted the rat and made Linguini catch Remy in a jar. "Dispose of it. **Go!**" Skinner ordered.

But Linguini didn't have the heart to toss the little rat into the river. He started talking to Remy instead. "What did you throw in there? Oregano?"

Remy shook his head. Linguini couldn't believe that Remy understood him!

"I can't cook, but you can, right?" Linguini asked. "They liked the soup. Do you think you can make it again?"

Remy nodded. He knew he could.

"Okay, we're together on this, right?" Linguini said as he let Remy out of the jar.

As soon as he was free, Remy ran for his life, **lickety-split**. But when the rat reached a safe distance, he glanced back. Linguini looked **sad** and alone.

Remy thought about it. This could be his big chance to become a chef! So he went back to his new friend.

Delighted, Linguini took the rat home to his tiny apartment.

The next morning, Remy greeted Linguini with a delectable omelet.

"Mmm. It's good," said Linguini, after taking a bite. "What did you put in this?" Remy pointed out the window to a neighbor's herb garden.

"Look. It's delicious. But don't steal. I'll buy some spices, okay?" Then Linguini glanced at the clock.

"Oh, no, we're gonna be late! C'mon, **Little Chef**!"

Back in the restaurant's kitchen, Linguini hid Remy in his shirt. The little rat tried to help Linguini with his cooking. He ran up one sleeve and down the other. Linguini giggled. But how else could Remy guide him to cook the soup? Remy bit hard on his friend's finger.

"Ow!" shouted Linguini. The other chefs thought he was crazy.

Linguini lurched into the food safe and closed the door. It was time to lay down some rules: no scampering, no scurrying, and no *biting*.

Suddenly, Skinner burst in and caught a glimpse of Remy.

"**The rat! I saw it!**" shouted the nasty little man.

Luckily, Linguini quickly hid Remy under his hat and ducked out.

"That was close," said Linguini.

Back in the bustling kitchen, Linguini was about to collide with the waiter, so Remy tugged his hair. Linguini jerked backward like a **puppet**! The young man was amazed. Could this be their new system?

Linguini and Remy went home to practice their cooking. Remy would guide Linguini by pulling his hair. Before long, Linguini was chopping, mixing, and pouring—all while blindfolded!

The next day at work, with Remy hidden under Linguini's hat, the odd duo made another pot of the delicious soup.

"Congratulations," sneered Skinner. "But you will need to know more than soup, boy, if you are to survive in my kitchen."

Skinner put Colette in charge of teaching Linguini.

Uh-oh! Colette was the toughest cook in the kitchen!

Back in his office, Skinner finally read the letter from Linguini's mother. It said that the famous Auguste Gusteau was Linguini's father. Nobody knew, not even Linguini—or Gusteau!

If it was true, the restaurant legally belonged to Linguini.

"This whole thing is highly suspect," Skinner told his lawyer, then asked him to investigate.

You see, Skinner had his own plans for the restaurant—and he didn't want Linguini ruining them!

In the kitchen, Colette taught Linguini how to keep his station clean, how to chop, and how to "listen" to **fresh bread**.

"Thanks for all of the advice about cooking," said Linguini.

"Thank **you** for taking it," replied Colette.

She was beginning to like Linguini, and he liked her, too.

For a few happy days, Linguini worked with Colette and watched the restaurant increase in popularity because of the now-famous soup.

One day, the waiter announced that a customer wanted a new dish from Linguini!

Furious and jealous, Skinner found the only recipe of Gusteau's that had failed. He ordered Linguini and Colette to cook it. Luckily, Remy forced Linguini to create a **special** sauce. Colette was angry that Linguini had not followed the recipe! But then they heard the news: the diner loved the meal!

That evening, Skinner invited Linguini into his office.
He really wanted to find out more about the **rat** that
kept appearing. Maybe the **rat** had something to do
with Linguini's cooking.

"Have you ever had a pet **rat**?" Skinner asked.

"Nope," Linguini replied.

"Did you work in a lab with **rats**?"

"Nope," said Linguini.

To Skinner's dismay, after many **rat** questions,
he did not get any information out of Linguini.

Outside, Remy was celebrating his success when a rustle behind the trash startled him.

"Remy!" called a familiar voice.

"Emile?" Remy replied.

The brothers had found each other at last! Remy took a step back. Emile had something disgusting in his mouth!

"What are you eating?" Remy asked.

"I don't really know," said Emile.

Remy returned to the kitchen and carefully selected delicious foods. It wasn't right to take them, and Remy knew it. But he wanted to give something special to his brother.

Once Emile tasted it, he couldn't wait to share it with the clan!

"Whoa, whoa, whoa!" said Remy. They had to keep the food a secret.

Emile agreed and led his long-lost brother
to the rats' new home in the sewers.

"We missed you!" Django cried, overjoyed.
"It hasn't been easy. Finding someone to
replace you as poison checker has been
a **disaster**."

Remy looked around at the rats' new home.
It had a jazz band, waiters, food. . . . But . . .

"I gotta, you know,
get back," Remy finally said.
"Get back to what?"
asked Django.
Remy explained that he had
friends, a job, a place to live.
"There's something I want you to see," Django
said. He led Remy up to a shop that specialized in
getting rid of rats for humans. "The world we live
in belongs to the enemy," said Django. "We look
out for our own kind, Remy. When all is said
and done, we're all we've got. Not humans."
Still, Remy returned to the restaurant.

The next morning, Colette confronted Linguini.
"I teach you a few tricks and then you blow past me?"
she said, upset from the night before. "I thought you
were different."

"Colette! Wait." Linguini began to confess. "It wasn't
me!" He nearly took off his cook's hat to reveal Remy!
"No, no!" Remy gasped, and yanked hard on
Linguini's hair. Linguini jerked forward and kissed
Colette. What a surprise! But it saved Remy's secret.

That day, in the office of Anton Ego, the most powerful restaurant critic in Paris, plans were afoot. Ego realized that despite his last **horrible** critique of Gusteau's restaurant, it had made an amazing comeback! So Ego was preparing for a new review on a **very grand** scale.

Meanwhile, Chef Skinner had just received some troubling news.

"The DNA matches," said Skinner's lawyer. Linguini was truly Gusteau's son—and therefore the rightful owner of the restaurant.

The lawyer assured the terrified Skinner that Linguini didn't know a thing and wouldn't find out before the restaurant was turned over to Skinner. So why worry?

After work, Linguini went for a ride with Colette on her motorcycle. In the wind, he lost his hat—and Remy! Linguini had forgotten all about the **little chef**, and Remy found himself on a dangerous, busy Paris street!

Exhausted and alone, Remy made his way back to the restaurant. That was when he heard Emile's voice.

"Little brother! We were afraid you weren't gonna show up!" Emile had brought friends along. Remy was **furious**!

"You told them? Emile, that's what I said not to do!"

But Remy knew that if he didn't give his brother's friends some food, they would blab his secret to the whole clan! So, reluctantly, he went to Skinner's office to find the key to the food safe.

Skinner's office was filled
with old pictures of Gusteau.
"Remy, what are you doing here?" one of the
photos asked him. "You aren't stealing food, are you?"
Remy felt terrible, but what else was he to do?
"Here it is." Remy found the key . . . and something
else. "Hey!"
It was Gusteau's will—and the letter from
Linguini's mother. This was news!
Linguini owned Gusteau's restaurant!

Just then, Skinner arrived! Terrified, Remy grabbed the papers and ran toward the river, with Skinner right behind him! Using the papers in his mouth as wings, Remy glided from one boat to another. Skinner jumped after him. And then—splash!—Skinner fell in. Furious, the little man floated as he watched Remy get away with the papers—and his plans for the restaurant.

By the time Skinner got back to Gusteau's, Linguini and Colette knew the whole story. Linguini fired the nasty chef!

The next day, Linguini was declared the legal **owner of Gusteau's**. Over the next few weeks, his fame spread all over Paris.

But Linguini wasn't paying attention to cooking anymore, and Remy didn't like it. Neither did Colette. Linguini even held a press conference in the dining room of the restaurant.

"My dad had his style of cooking, and I have mine," Linguini boasted to the reporters.

As the cameras clicked away, Anton Ego arrived and gave his warning: "I will return tomorrow night with **high expectations**."

When Linguini finally entered the kitchen again, Remy felt so angry that he yanked Linguini's hair, *hard*! Linguini stormed out the back door and waved his finger in the rat's face.

"You take a break, Little Chef. I'm not your **puppet**!"

Hidden, Skinner watched the whole argument. He confirmed it at last:

"The rat is the cook!"

Meanwhile, Emile showed up at Gusteau's with the whole hungry rat colony. Remy was so angry with Linguini that he showed them the food safe and told them to take what they wanted.

"Oh, this is great, son!" said Django.

That was when Linguini returned to apologize.

"You're stealing from me?" a startled Linguini asked Remy angrily when he saw all the rats. "I thought **you were my friend**. I trusted you! Get out and don't come back!"

Remy felt terrible. The next day,
he returned to the restaurant alley, intending
to help Linguini cook for Ego. Instead, he got
caught in a **trap** that Skinner had set!

Skinner knew that without Remy, Linguini would
fail. Skinner also called the health inspector and
reported *rats*!

Luckily, Emile and Django arrived and busted the
cage to get Remy out.

Remy boldly walked into the kitchen through the back door. The chefs took one look and yelled, "Raaat!!!"

"Don't touch him!" shouted Linguini. "The truth is I have no talent at all. But this rat—he's the one behind the recipes. He's the cook. The real cook."

From the shadows, Django watched his son with the human.

The cooks said nothing. And one by one, they walked out—even Colette. Linguini retreated to his office, leaving Remy alone.

Django stepped out of the shadows. "I was wrong about you. About him." Remy knew then that his father was proud of him.

Suddenly, the health inspector arrived!

"Stop him!" yelled Django. Like lightning, a team of rats went after the health inspector. The rest climbed into the dishwasher, then emerged clean and ready to prepare, roast, grill, and create sauces.

When Linguini saw the cooking commotion, he knew exactly what he needed to do.

"We need someone to wait tables," he said. Tonight, Linguini would be the waiter! Then Colette came back, just in time to help. But when Remy selected the recipe, she shook her head.

"This dish is humble. Ego is not. **Are you sure?**"

Remy nodded, so Colette got to work. Of course, Remy chose which spices went into the pot!

Linguini sped the steaming stew out to Ego.

Skinner had sneaked into the restaurant in disguise, hoping to see Linguini fail. "Ratatouille?" the nasty little chef mumbled. "They must be joking!"

But to Ego, this was no joke. The delicious **ratatouille** brought back memories from his childhood—a bad memory of getting hurt and a good memory of a mother's love and her delicious cooking.

Ego insisted on giving his compliments to the chef. Linguini refused to take the credit. Instead, he waited until the last customers left and then introduced Anton Ego to the real chef: Remy.

Ego left without saying a word.

The next morning, Ego gave the restaurant a five-star review in the paper: *"It is difficult to imagine more humble origins than those of the genius now cooking at Gusteau's, who is, in this critic's opinion, nothing less than the finest chef in France. I shall be returning soon, hungry for more."*

Unfortunately, Gusteau's restaurant was closed down by the health inspector. You see, there was a little problem: rats. But soon a new bistro, La Ratatouille, opened. It became famous for its delicious food—and not as well known for one special little chef and some tiny customers.

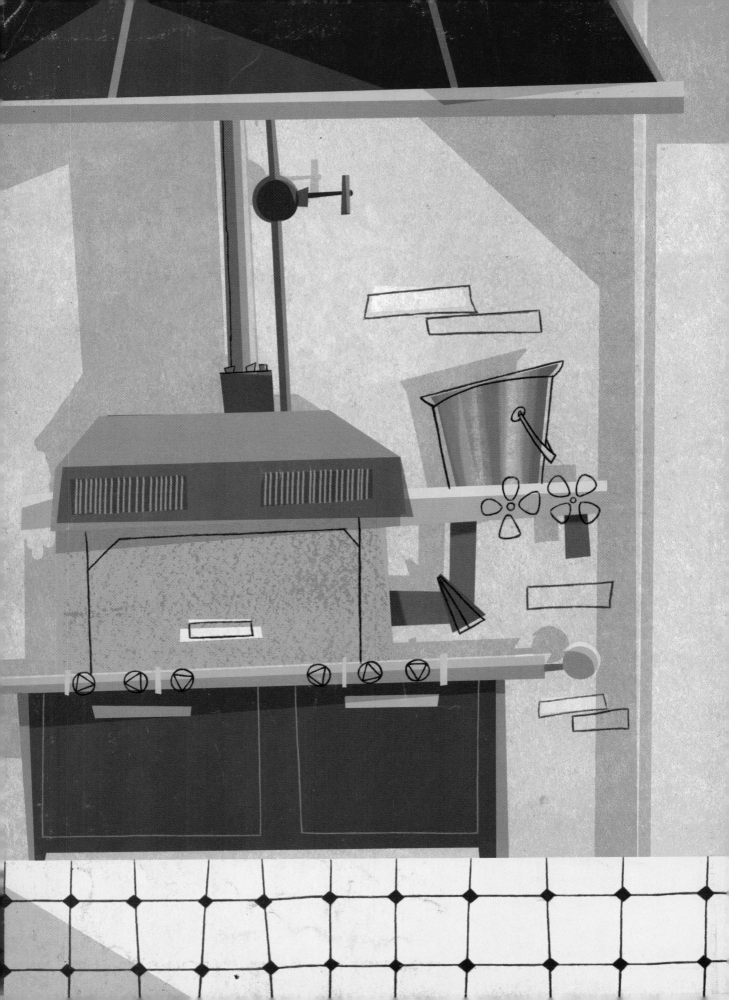